Incredulità!

Utrolig!

NICHT WAHR!

Incroyable!

Ja nie wiezy!

¡No es posible!

HINDI KAPANIPANIWALA!

Etă nivazmózhna!

Mangel på tro!

Nie możliwie!

Incrível!

NICHT WAHR!

Would you believe!

Det är otroligt!

Incredulità!

Utrolig!

Incrível!

Ja nie wiezy!

Incroyable!

¡No es posible!

HINDI KAPANIPANIWALA!

Etă nivaz

Mangel på tro!

Nie możliwie

Incrível!

Would you believe!

NICHT WAHR!

Det är otroligt!

D1716446

More... Would You Believe?

By ISAAC ASIMOV

Illustrated by Pat Schories

Publishers • GROSSET & DUNLAP • New York

Above & Below

The moon is always falling. It has a sideways motion of its own that balances its falling motion. It therefore stays in a closed orbit around the Earth, never falling altogether and never escaping altogether.

Jupiter is two and one half times larger than all the other planets, satellites, asteroids, and comets of our solar system *combined*.

Jupiter's Great Red Spot is 25,000 miles wide. The spot may be the vortex of a hurricane that has been whirling for at least seven centuries.

Because the air at the end of the day is generally dustier than it is at the beginning of the day, the setting sun is redder than the rising sun.

Millions of meteorites fall against the outer limits of the atmosphere every day and are burned to nothing by the friction.

To go on the lunar day, merely adjust your watch to lose two minutes and five seconds every hour.

In the constellation Cygnus, there is a double star, one of whose components has such a high surface gravity that light cannot escape from it. It is Cygnus X-1, which many astronomers believe to be the first "black hole" to be detected.

As late as 1820, the universe was thought by European scientists to be 6,000 years old. It is now thought to be between 15 billion and 20 billion years old.

There has been a blue moon. When a large amount of fine dust was sent into the upper atmosphere by huge Canadian forest fires in 1950, the dust caused a blue coloring in various parts of the world. Cars turned their headlights on in the daytime, and at least one daytime baseball game was played under lights. In some places, people even reported a blue sun. The phenomenon lasted at least two days.

The driest place on Earth is Calama, in the Atacama Desert in Chile. Not a drop of rain has been seen there.

Lightning is more likely than not to strike twice in the same place. Like all electric currents or discharges, lightning follows the path of least resistance.

Through the largest telescope on Earth, and in the most favorable circumstances, it would not be possible to see an object on the moon much smaller than a half mile across.

A manned rocket reaches the moon in less time than it took a stagecoach to travel the length of England.

Astronauts circling the Earth may get to see 16 sunrises and 16 sunsets every "day."

Until the time of Galileo, an argument used with potent effect was that if the Earth moved, and if it indeed rotated on its axis, the birds would be blown away, clouds would be left behind, and buildings would tumble.

A "shell" of TV and radio signals carrying old *Gangbusters* and *Lone Ranger* and *Howdy Doody* radio and television programs is expanding through the cosmos at the speed of light, sweeping past the stars.

Bamboo may grow three feet in twenty-four hours.

So dense, so impenetrable is the spruce-treed forest of the vast Canadian Lakes district, in central Canada, that winter snow stays on top of the trees, like a blanket, and the forest floor stays bare.

It takes more than two tons of South African rock to produce an ounce of gold.

The amount of gold dissolved in the oceans is nearly 9 million tons, about 180 times the amount of gold dug out of mines in the entire history of humanity. The gold in the oceans is too diffuse to be extractable at a profit.

In early Egyptian history, silver was more valued than gold, because silver was found less often in nugget form.

Most healthy adults can go without eating anything for a month or longer. But they must drink at least two quarts of water a day.

Perfectly still water can be lowered to temperatures several degrees lower than the freezing point (32° F) and remain liquid.

Each time the tide rises, every one of us loses a fraction of an ounce, but the weight is regained as the tide falls. We are affected by these tidal waves, just as the ocean is, because of the water and salt content of our bodies. The land and air are affected as well by the tides. Every time the water rises in a ten foot tide, the continents rise about six inches, and the atmosphere bulges many miles.

The temperature can become so cold in eastern Siberia that the moisture in a person's breath can freeze in the air and fall to the earth with soft crackling or whispering sounds.

The hardness of ice is similar to that of concrete.

Water freezes faster if it is cooled rapidly from a relatively warm temperature than if it is cooled at the same rate from a lower temperature.

A catastrophic temperature drop is not needed to get an ice age under way. The drop need only be enough to allow a little more snow to fall during a slightly colder winter than can be melted by a succeeding, slightly cooler summer.

The Amazon River has 1,100 tributary streams.

Great Ideas

After the first moon walk, in 1969, Pan American Airlines began accepting reservations for commercial flights to the moon, dates and time unspecified. More than 80,000 requests poured in immediately.

Mark Twain secured a patent in 1873 for a self-pasting scrapbook. A series of blank pages was coated with gum.

Charles Dickens believed that a good night's sleep was only possible if the bed was aligned from north to south. In this manner, he thought, the magnetic currents would flow straight through the recumbent body.

The roots of Einstein's intellectual development of relativity grew, he said, from his wonder at what light waves would look like to him if he moved as fast as they did.

As a boy in Scotland, Alexander Graham Bell made a talking doll that said, "Mama."

Tired of pounding the pavements looking for a job, Humphrey O'Sullivan sat down one day and invented the rubber heel.

The story of Newton and the apple is one legend that's true. Newton described it himself. He saw an apple fall from a tree to the ground at a time when the crescent moon was in the evening sky. He pondered on whether or not the moon was held in the grip of the same force the apple was—the rest is history. However, there is one part of the story that is *not* true. When it fell, the apple did not hit Newton on the head.

An artificial hand, with fingers moved by cogwheels and levers, was designed in 1551 by a Frenchman, Ambroise Paré. It even enabled a handless calvalryman to grasp the reins of a horse.

Though he had never seen a clock, Benjamin Banneker (1731-1806) was able to make a clock that ran accurately for a score of years. Banneker was a mathematician, astronomer, surveyor of the District of Columbia, and almanac publisher.

Coal dust sprayed by aircraft over Russian fields absorbs the early spring sunshine. The resulting warmth melts the snow a little sooner.

The Navajo language was used successfully as a code by the United States in World War II.

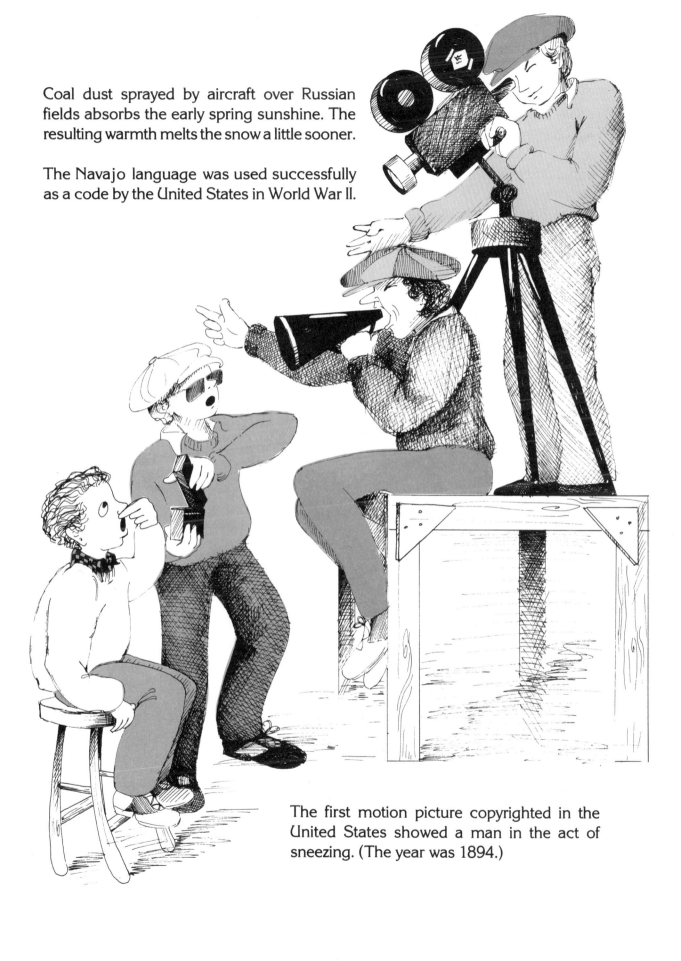

The first motion picture copyrighted in the United States showed a man in the act of sneezing. (The year was 1894.)

The snow-capped "land of the thunder drag-on"—Bhutan, north of India—issued a post-age stamp that is actually a tiny phonograph record. It plays, naturally, the Bhutanese national anthem.

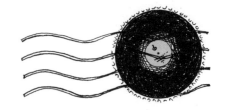

Henry Ford was convinced that the soybean was a promising raw material. He was sure that it could be converted into products with commercial value. Ford once appeared at a convention with his entire attire, except for his shoes, having been produced from soybeans.

Cat's cradle is one of the most universal games. It is played in almost every culture. What is sometimes a puzzle to ethnologists is that widely scattered peoples—Maoris of New Zealand, North American Indians, Arctic Eskimos, and Africans, for instance—make figures of string between their hands that are exactly the same.

Ketchup was once sold as a patent medicine. In the 1830s it enjoyed a measure of popularity in the United States as *Dr. Miles' Compound Extract of Tomato.*

To keep your feet warm, put on a hat. Of all body heat that is lost, 80 percent escapes through the head.

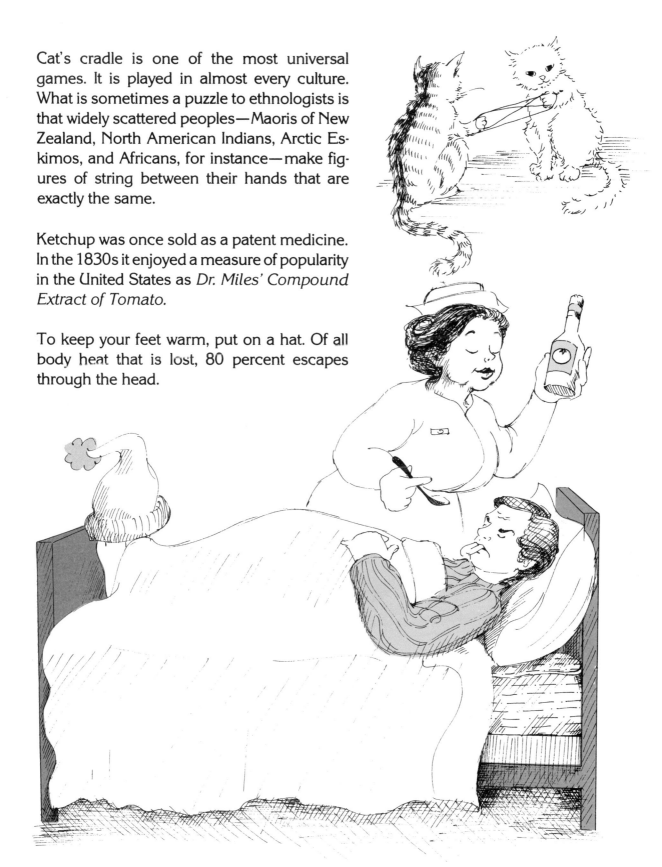

To prove that girls could master such subjects as mathematics and philosophy without detracting from their health or charm, Emma Hart Willard founded the Troy (New York) Female Seminary, in 1821.

Based on the rate at which knowledge is growing, it can be speculated that by the time today's child reaches the age of fifty, 97 percent of everything known in the world at that time will have been learned since his birth.

The composer John Cage's Imaginary Landscape No. 4 (1953) never sounds the same way twice. It is scored for twelve radios tuned at random.

In the mid 1960s, the motion picture director-producer Stanley Kubrick wanted from Lloyd's of London an insurance policy protecting against losses should extraterrestrial intelligence be discovered before completion and release of his motion picture, *2001: A Space Odyssey.* Lloyd's didn't take the chance.

Way Back When

By the eighteenth century, apple pie had become so popular a dessert in America that Yale college served it every night at supper, and did so for more than a century.

When tea was first introduced in the American colonies, many housewives, in their ignorance, served the tea leaves with sugar or syrup after throwing away the water in which they had been boiled.

The modern dinner plate is a fairly recent development. Until the fifteenth century, it was customary to eat on a thick slice of stale bread, called a "trencher," that soaked up the juice.

In 1418, women's headgear was so tall that the doorways of the royal castle at Vincennes, France, had to be raised, on the orders of the queen, to allow ladies of the court to pass through without ducking.

There was no soap in the ancient Mediterranean world. Olive oil was used not only for cooking but for washing the body.

The era of the Middle Ages has been described as "1000 years without a bath." Bathing was rare in Europe at that time, largely because the Christian church considered it a sin to expose the body, even to oneself. It was not until 1641 that soap was manufactured in England. Religion had become less oppressive, but government harassment in the form of restrictions and taxes on the soap making industry caused the soap business to develop slowly.

In seventeenth and eighteenth century America, women were employed in all of the same occupations men were, and women earned equal pay. A female blacksmith charged the same as a man to shoe a horse. Women sextons and printers were paid the same rate as men. Women were silversmiths, gunsmiths, shipwrights, and undertakers.

When the first escalator, or "inclined elevator," was installed in the department store Harrod's in London (near the turn of the century), brandy was served to passengers who felt faint.

In 1695, two scientists obtained a diamond from a rich patron and heated it by using a lens to focus light upon it. The diamond disappeared. Diamond is made of carbon, and burns just as coal will when it is heated strongly enough.

Twenty-one people were killed by a wave of molasses in Boston, Massachusetts in 1919. Over 2 million gallons of melted sugar, weighing 13,500 tons, had been stored in a tank in the harbor. The tank ruptured, for reasons never fully determined, and the wave, cresting at fifty feet, swallowed eight buildings.

Early guns took so long to load and fire that bows and arrows—in trained hands—were twelve times more efficient.

Though Theodore Roosevelt's famous attack in Cuba in the Spanish-American War is referred to as the charge of the "Rough Riders," the troops were not mounted.

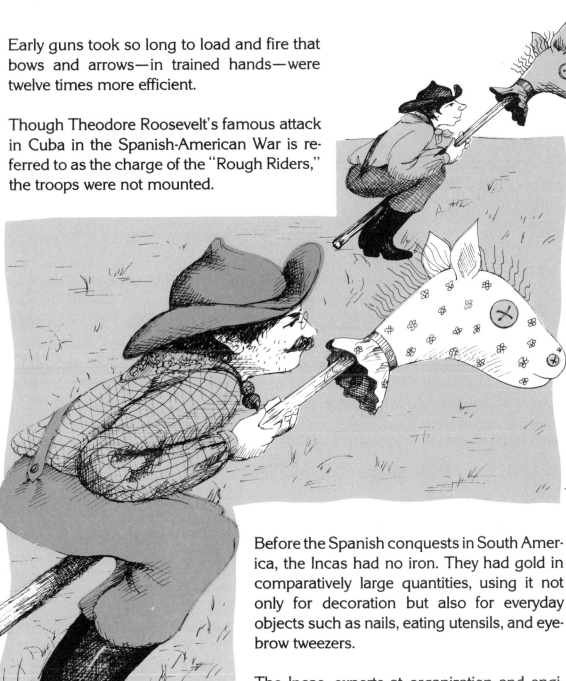

Before the Spanish conquests in South America, the Incas had no iron. They had gold in comparatively large quantities, using it not only for decoration but also for everyday objects such as nails, eating utensils, and eyebrow tweezers.

The Incas, experts at organization and engineering, did not have wheels, arches, or writing. At the height of their power, before the Spanish conquest in 1532, the Incas ruled the entire area in South America from Quito, Ecuador, to the Rio Maule, Chile. Their empire was centered at Cuzco, Peru.

Secret codes and ciphers are thousands of years old. Many prominent persons throughout history have written in ciphers for diplomatic and military reasons; they include Julius Caesar, Charlemagne, Alfred the Great, Mary Queen of Scots, and Louis XIV.

During their first winter in the New World—and a rugged winter it was—the Pilgrims secretly buried their dead in Cole's Hill in Plymouth. The reason for the secrecy: they did not want the Indians to know how much the settlement had shrunk in population.

In July, 1585, 108 Englishmen landed at Roanoke Island off the coast of North Carolina. Sponsored by Sir Walter Raleigh, the settlers built a fort and houses, planted crops, and sought gold. Hurricanes and hostile Indians forced them to return to England within a year. In 1587, another 118 colonists arrived, among them the parents of Virginia Dare, the first English baby to be born in the New World. The leader of the colony, John White, sailed back to England after a few weeks to get more provisions. When he returned to Roanoke in 1591, he found it deserted. The word "CROATOAN" was carved on a tree, and to this day, no one knows what happened to the settlers.

Some dinosaurs were as small as hens.

Until the 1850s, shoes were made by hand and most were "straight"; they could be worn on either foot. There were two widths: fat and slim; most Americans wore slim. The concept and production of left and right shoes came in with machines.

Using chemicals to get "high" isn't as new as one might think. Nitrous oxide was discovered in 1800. When inhaled, it was found to give a giddy, intoxicated feeling and to release the emotions. People laughed inanely, and it was called "laughing gas". For a while, parties were organized at which people sat around inhaling its fumes.

An authentic lost weapon is Greek fire, which the Byzantine Empire used on several occasions between the seventh and ninth centuries to defend Constantinople against attacking Muslims. Constantinople might have fallen but for Greek fire, and conceivably the Muslims might have taken over a weak and divided Europe. To this day, we don't know exactly what the "recipe" for Greek fire was. All we know is that it burned all the more fiercely when wet, and that it could be floated toward the enemy's wooden ships.

Places & Faces

The Indians of Tierra del Fuego, at the tip of South America, near Antarctica, wore no clothes to protect themselves from the sleet-filled air and icy waters.

Having survived a barrel ride over Niagara Falls that broke "nearly every bone" in his body, in 1911, Bobby Leech embarked on a lecture tour around the world. In New Zealand, he slipped on a banana peel and died of complications from the fall.

The celebrated seventeenth century pirate William Kidd was a wealthy landowner in New York.

Isaac Newton's only recorded utterance while he was a member of Parliament was a request to open the window.

By the age of twenty-five, he had been expelled from the army and was disgraced, despondent, without funds, and apparently without a future. The man was Napoleon (1769-1821). One year later, he was the youngest general in the French Army, and began winning victories with ragged troops that were at the point of starvation.

Mark Twain was born in 1835 when Halley's comet appeared. He predicted that he would die when Halley's comet next returned to scare everyone—and he did, in 1910. The comet will next return in 1986. The last time the comet was seen superstitious people bought anticomet pills at $1 a box.

The Russian composer Sergei Prokofiev composed an opera, *The Giant*, when he was only seven years old—using only the white keys.

Beethoven was half-deaf most of his life. He was completely deaf when he composed his greatest work, the Ninth Symphony.

There were at least fifty-two musicians in the family of Johann Sebastian Bach.

The Apache Indian chief Geronimo, after surrendering in 1886 and being imprisoned in Florida and Alabama, became a farmer and a member of the Dutch Reformed Church on a military reservation in Oklahoma. He was eventually expelled by the church for gambling.

D.H. Lawrence, one of the most original and controversial writers of the twentieth century, had a fancy for removing his clothes and climbing mulberry trees.

As though he didn't have everything else going for him, Leonardo da Vinci was described by people who knew him as the "most beautiful man who ever lived."

Vincent Van Gogh is known to have sold only one painting.

The parents of one of the few five-star generals in United States history, Dwight D. Eisenhower, were pacifists.

Francis Bacon (1561-1626) the Elizabethan champion of the scientific method, died in pursuit of a better way of preserving food. He had caught a severe cold while attempting to preserve a chicken by filling it with snow.

Henry Cavendish, one of the great scientists of the 1700s was painfully shy and could barely speak to one person—never to two. He was so afraid, (or shy, or something) in the presence of women that he communicated with his female servants by notes only. If one crossed his path in his house, she was fired on the spot. He built a separate entrance to his house so he could come and go without meeting anyone. In the end, he insisted on dying alone.

Helen Keller (1880-1968) blind and deaf from an early age, developed her sense of smell so finely that she could identify friends by their personal odors.

The fear that he might conceal a joke in it was one of the reasons that Benjamin Franklin was not entrusted by his peers with the assignment of writing the Declaration of Independence.

Rudyard Kipling spent five of the happiest years of his life in Brattleboro, Vermont, in the 1890s. So that he could get outdoor exercise in the winter, he invented snow golf, painting his golf balls red so that they could be located in the snow.

Napoleon suffered from ailurophobia, the fear of cats.

Cyrano de Bergerac really lived (from about 1620 to 1655) big nose, dueling, and all. He was a poet, a dramatist, and a science fiction writer. He wrote of voyages to the moon and to the sun and was the first person to suggest (in 1650) the one method that could carry us into space—rockets.

A woman, Elizabeth Van Lew, was rated by General Grant as his most effective secret agent during the Civil War. Known as "Crazy Bet," this supposedly demented daughter of a well-to-do Richmond merchant passed information to Union commanders and arranged daring prison escapes for Union soldiers, hiding the fugitives in a secret room in her mansion overlooking the James River.

When he was already President of the United States and his mother was past eighty years of age, Franklin Roosevelt remarked that he had never in his life gone out of doors without his mother calling after him, "Franklin! Are you sure you're dressed warmly enough?"

Two British prime ministers, Clement Attlee and Winston Churchill, when they were children, had the same governess.

Though they were only five and three years old, Susan and Deborah Tripp, two sisters in the United States, in 1829, weighed 205 and 124 pounds, respectively.

Eskimos use refrigerators to keep food from freezing.

Henry David Thoreau (1817-62) the American author and naturalist who spent more than two years in close harmony with nature, leading a near solitary life free of materialistic pursuits, built his hermitage cabin on the shore of Walden Pond near Concord, Massachusetts. The cabin was only 500 yards from the railroad tracks connecting Fitchburg and Boston.

In addition to silversmithing, Paul Revere practiced dentistry in colonial Boston. He learned the craft from a surgeon dentist and advertised himself as being prepared to fix loose false teeth and to clean teeth.

New York City's administrative code still requires that hitching posts be located in front of City Hall so that reporters can tie up their horses.

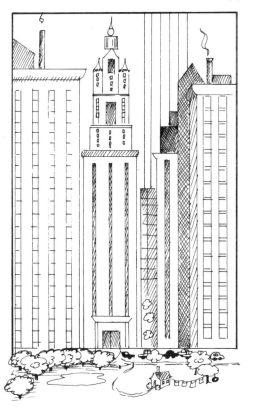

Central Park in the heart of Manhattan, in New York City, is so beautifully designed and its features so finely accentuated that it would seem that nature herself had been the designer. Not so. The 840 acres were a marshy area littered with filth and shanties when Frederick Law Olmsted and Calvert Vaux, in 1857, began shaping a park that now serves as the model for other public areas in the United States.

Oak Island, off the coast of Nova Scotia has a mysterious deep shaft that has resisted exploration because the water cannot be pumped out. All that has been discerned is that the shaft was dug and lined with logs in the eighteenth century by an unknown band of men.

There are 2,500,000 rivets in the Eiffel Tower.

The height of the 984-foot tall (usually) Eiffel Tower varies, depending on the temperature, by as much as six inches.

Wheels

There are a half a million more automobiles in Los Angeles than there are people.

Courts of law in the United States devote more than half their time to cases involving automobiles.

The first automobile to cross the United States took fifty-two days in 1903, to go from San Francisco to New York.

One third of all the automobiles in New York City, Boston, and Chicago in 1900 were electric cars, with batteries rather than gasoline engines.

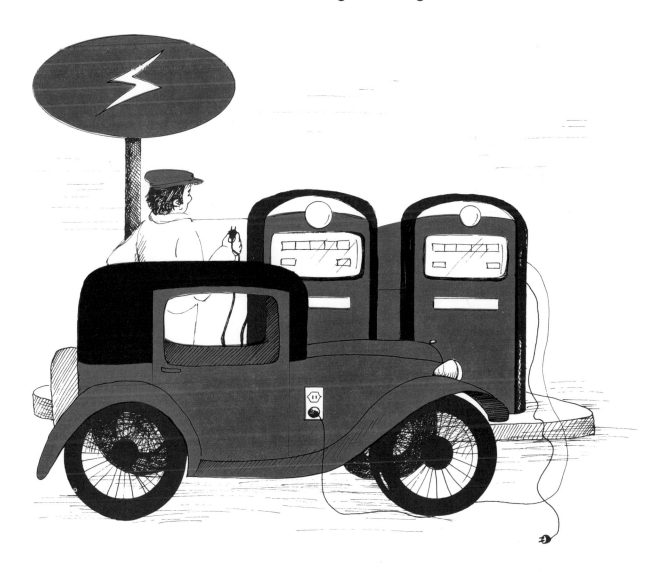

Robert Moses, the planner largely responsible for many of New York's bridges, tunnels, and parkways, never learned to drive an automobile.

The Soviets are buying skateboards from the United States—but not for recreational purposes. They see them as an answer to some of the country's transportation needs because the boards are less expensive than bicycles and require little storage space. The first boards went to school instructors so they could teach pupils how to ride them.

Fur, Feathers, Fins & Feelers

Snails sleep a lot. In addition to several months of winter hibernation, they crawl into their shells to get out of the hot sun, which dries them, or heavy rain, which waterlogs them. Desert snails may even doze for three or four years.

The ancestors of the horse were only about a foot tall 60 million years ago.

The Romans were so fond of eating dormice that the upper class raised them domestically. The rodents were kept in specially designed cages and fed a mixture of nuts.

Ben Franklin wanted the turkey, not the eagle to be the U.S. national symbol. He considered the eagle "a bird of bad moral character" because it lives by "sharping and robbing".

The grizzly bear can run as fast as the average horse.

Thinking that its parents were a camel and a leopard, the Europeans once called the animals a camelopard. Today, it's called a giraffe.

At birth, a panda is smaller than a mouse and weighs about four ounces.

Bats are the only mammals that are able to fly. The flying squirrel can only do what the gliding oppossum does—glide for short distances.

Chimpanzees have been trained to have recognition vocabularies of 100 to 200 words. They can also distinguish among different grammatical patterns.

The fastest dog, the greyhound, can reach speeds of up to 41.7 miles per hour. The breed was known to exist in ancient Egypt 6,000 years ago.

There are more kinds of insects in the world today than the total of all the other kinds of animals put together.

A seeing-eye dog, or any dog trained to guide the blind, cannot tell a red light from a green one. When it leads its master across the street, it watches the traffic flow to tell when it is safe to cross.

There are locusts that have an adult life span of only a few weeks or so, after having lived in the ground as grubs for fifteen years.

To make a one-pound comb of honey, bees must collect nectar from about two million flowers.

A parrot's beak can close with a force of 350 pounds per square inch.

Second most numerous of living things—second only to insects—are mollusks (soft-bodied animals with hard shells).

To survive, every bird must eat at least half its own weight in food every day. Young birds need even more. A young robin, for example, eats as much as fourteen feet of earthworms a day.

Many songbirds learn to sing by listening to adult birds of the same species. If separated from the adults, they develop unintelligible warbles, rather than normal song patterns. But if taught the song of another species, a bird can often pass the foreign language on to its offspring. In one experiment, a male bullfinch, raised by a female canary, learned the canary's song to perfection. When it was later mated to a female bullfinch, its children, and later its grandchildren, could sing like a canary.

Fish can be susceptible to seasickness. Artificial "storm waves," made in a glass bowl, in a scientific study, resulted in seasick goldfish.

A starfish can be cut into sizable chunks and each piece will grow into a completely whole starfish.

Not all fish live only in the water. Walking catfish, mudskippers, and flying fish, among many species, can live on land.

Sharks can be dangerous even before they are born. One scientist, Stewart Springer, was bitten by a sand tiger shark embryo while he was examining its pregnant mother.

Sideshow performers in ancient Greece used to amaze their audiences by pressing a spot on a goat's neck—pinching off the artery leading to the brain—and causing it to go to sleep. Releasing the pressure would allow the goat to wake up again. (The trick still works today.)

Rin Tin Tin, for years the most famous dog in the world, was born to a war-dog mother in a German trench in France in World War I. Deserted when the Germans retreated, the German shepherd puppy was found by an American officer, who happened to be a police dog trainer from California. He trained Rin Tin Tin when they returned home. The dog was so intelligent that he came to the notice of Warner Brothers, which signed him up for what turned out to be a long career as one of the biggest box-office draws of the silent screen.

Dolphins can, and do, kill barracudas with one snap of their jaws, and kill sharks by merely ramming them with their snouts. However, dolphins have never been known to attack humans. This is considered evidence of their intelligence.

Both Scarlatti and Chopin were inspired by cats. When Scarlatti's cat struck certain notes on the keys of his harpsichord, one by one, with its paws, Scarlatti proceeded to write, "The Cat's Fugue," a fugue for harpsichord in D minor. While Chopin was composing Waltz No. 3 in F major, his cat ran across the keys of the piano, amusing Chopin so much that he tried for the same sounds in what is called "The Cat's Waltz."

Bits & Pieces

Ninety-nine percent of all forms of life that ever existed on earth are now extinct.

The rare metal gallium melts at 86° F. It is safe to touch; if you hold a piece of it in your hand and wait, it will melt.

A person's hair cannot turn white overnight because of some terrible tragedy or frightening experience—or for any other reason.

You won't get a bellyache from eating a green apple as long as you chew it completely. The stomach doesn't know the difference between ripe and unripe apples.

The skin of the adult human body weighs about six pounds.

Honey is used as a center for golf balls and in antifreeze mixtures.

A perpetual motion machine would violate the laws of thermodynamics. Nobody has ever succeeded in producing one; nobody ever will.

The formidable looking black rhinoceros, weighing over a ton, is considered the most easily tameable animal in Africa. Once penned, he becomes so gentle that he will eat out of his keeper's hand, and will come on call to have his ears rubbed.

England and Portugal have never been at war with each other. It's probably the longest unbroken peace between nations in the world.

With both sides willing, the Roman Empire and Persia signed "The Endless Peace," treaty in 553, A.D. They were back at war with each other within seven years.

Bacteria, the tiniest free-living cells, are so small that a single drop of liquid may contain 50 million of them.

Icelanders read more books per capita than any other people in the world.

Copies of all the millions of books, (over 16.5 million) in the Library of Congress could be reduced page by page to photochromatic microimages and the lot could be stored in six four-drawer filing cabinets.

The most common name in the world is neither Ching nor John; it's Muhammad.

The Metropolitan Museum of Art, in New York, houses the world's largest collection of baseball cards: 200,000.

Man has tiny bones once meant for a tail and unworkable muscles once meant to move his ears.

A boomerang cannot return to the thrower after hitting anything.

Kernels of popcorn were found in the graves of pre-Columbian Indians.

A device invented as a primitive steam engine by the Greek engineer Hero, about the time of the birth of Christ, is used today as a rotating lawn sprinkler.

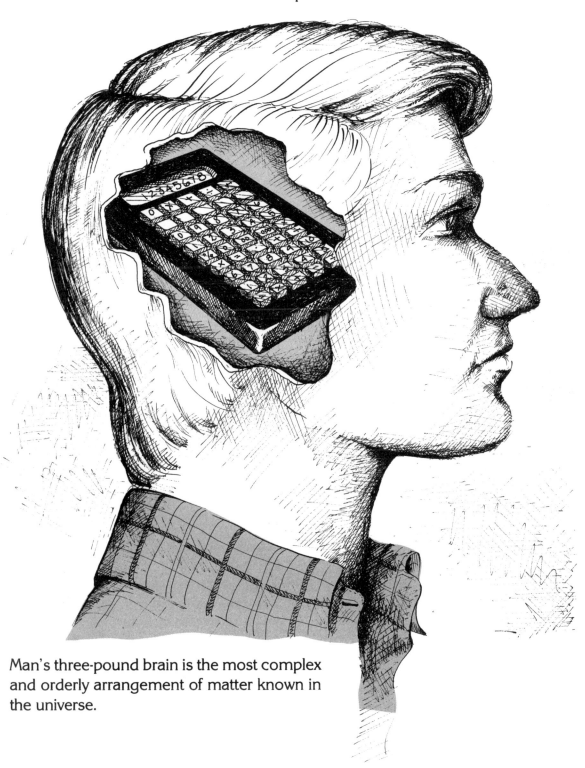

Man's three-pound brain is the most complex and orderly arrangement of matter known in the universe.

A chip of silicon a quarter inch square has the capacity of the original 1949 ENIAC computer, which occupied a city block.

No secret, now-forgotten preservatives were involved in preparing an Egyptian mummy. Common substances were used—such as beeswax, oil, and salt. The procedure, though, could be complicated and take up to seventy days. To be made waterproof, the body was wrapped in bandages, then smeared with wax. The Persian word for wax was *mum*. The Arab word was *mumia*. To us, it's now "mummy."

In and around Zion, a little town in Illinois, on the shore of Lake Michigan about forty miles north of Chicago, there are hundreds, perhaps thousands, of people who believe the Earth is not round. They are supporters of a theory, proposed in the early 1900s by Wilbur Glenn Voliva, that the Earth is flat. There are also people today who believe the world is hollow and open at the poles. There are some who even believe the Earth is on the inside of a hollow sphere.

Mangel på tro!

Ětá nívazmózhna!

Incrível!

Nie możliwie!

Would you believe!

NICHT WAHR!

Det är otroligt!

Incredulità!

Utrolig!

Nie możliwie!

Incroyable!

Ja nie wiezy!

HINDI KAPANIPANIWALA!

¡No es posible!

Mangel på tro!

Ětá nívazmózhna!

Incrível!

Nie możliwie!

Would you believe!

NICHT WAHR!

Det är otroligt!

Incredulità!

Utrolig!

¡No es posible!

Incroyable!

Ja nie wiezy!

HINDI KAPANIPANIWALA!

¡No es posible!